Fairy Tales for Life

Fairy Tales for Life

A Collection of Fourteen Original Short Stories

Linda Champion

With Illustrations by Rose Fante

Two Harbors Press
Minneapolis, MN

Two Harbors Press
322 First Avenue N, 5th floor
Minneapolis, MN 55401
612.455.2293
www.TwoHarborsPress.com

ISBN-13: 978-1-62652-938-0
LCCN: 2014911484

Distributed by Itasca Books

Cover Design and Typeset by James Arneson

Printed in the United States of America

Dedicated to my husband, Kenneth Champion

CONTENTS

Acknowledgments ~ ix

Introduction ~ xi

The Storyteller ~ 1

The Dragon Slayer ~ 5

The Duet of Love ~ 9

The Liar Family ~ 13

The Love Child ~ 19

The Hermit ~ 25

The Dance of Love ~ 29

The Clock ~ 35

The Friends ~ 41

A Mother's Love ~ 49

The Heart ~ 55

The Last Letter ~ 61

True Love ~ 69

The Wonders of Fairy Land ~ 75

Epilogue ~ 79

About the Author ~ 80

About the Illustrator ~ 81

Acknowledgments

I want to thank my husband, Kenneth Champion, for his loving support of my fairy tales. His belief in me has been my greatest treasure. I also appreciate my family and friends: Margaret Oakley, Nathan Champion, Tamera Barnes, Tania Kanakis, Jeanette DeWald, Rebecca Nesbitt, Chris Nesbitt, Marshall Nesbitt, Martha Cramer, Claire Forehand, Deb Watkins, Jo Lotz, Wendy Murrill, and Lora Nishimura. They cheered me on, and their insightful comments were gratefully received. In addition, I want to thank my illustrator, Rose Fante, who made my stories come to life with her beautiful drawings. Lastly, I am grateful to all the people at Two Harbors Press who helped make my personal fairy tale come true.

Introduction

So what is a fairy tale? Well, there is a lot of disagreement about this. Just to give us all a general understanding, a fairy tale is a type of short story that can include a whole host of imaginary creatures and usually has some magic thrown in for good measure. Oddly enough, the only detail on which most experts agree is that a fairy tale doesn't have to include a fairy. An elf or a talking clock will do.

There is another matter to take care of. Some of you may be thinking that you are too old for fairy tales. I would argue that these stories have a universal appeal for all ages, especially if you look below the surface. Fairy tales often reveal themes that are more mature or serious and darker in their telling. In fact, when I wrote *Fairy Tales for Life: A Collection of Fourteen Original Short Stories*, I had an adult audience in mind, although many of my stories are also appropriate for younger readers.

Probably what is most fascinating about these stories is the limitless use of imagination. A fox can talk and all kinds of other amazing things can happen, and at the same time these characters can have some very humanlike qualities and the events can relate to some real human experiences. And, in addition, the writer has a smorgasbord of literary devices to play with. In short, there is more freedom for a writer of fairy tales than with any other literary genre.

The reader also has the opportunity to use his or her imagination in the reading of these tales. Since these are short stories, the reader has the freedom to fill in all the missing details and has more room to interpret the story. So, fairy tales offer an equal opportunity for creative input by both the writer and the reader.

Why did I write these stories? Well, like all writers, I wanted to express some thoughts about life. For one thing, I have been concerned about the importance of love and how it can be lost. It is the most precious thing in the world, but it is often ignored, abused, or totally forgotten.

My purpose and hope is that my stories will stir the heart of the reader to think about this and some other important issues in life. A very good friend of mine described my writing as stories about life. This is probably the best description of this literary effort.

So, if you are a more mature reader, don't assume that you have been relegated to the children's nursery as you read these stories. Think of it this way: you have found fourteen original tales that will take you down a path leading to some of the great challenges of life. Enjoy the journey!

Linda Champion

"'Let me tell you a story,' began the Storyteller."

The Storyteller

"Let me tell you a story," began the Storyteller. And with these words, the man charmed the people gathered around him with yet another one of his many beautiful narratives. He was known for his great wisdom and understanding of people. He was, as everyone called him, the Storyteller.

When the Storyteller had finished his tale, he left the people and began to walk, enjoying the pretty countryside that surrounded him. As he strolled along, he noticed that several couples languished on the grass among the brightly colored flowers. He smiled to himself. Love seemed to be in bloom everywhere. He continued on his way.

After awhile, he found himself entering a grove of apple trees. "What a wonderful piece of luck," he mused. "There's nothing better than an apple to take the edge off an empty stomach."

He hurried to the nearest tree and reached up for an apple. Just as he did, he heard someone cry, "Sir! You are stepping on me!"

The Storyteller looked down and saw the startled face of a young woman. In his great haste, he had failed to notice the woman sitting beneath the tree.

"I beg your pardon, young lady," said the Storyteller. "I guess my hunger got the better of me."

"Well, you are pardoned," answered the woman, "but, sir, do you always rush in without looking?"

"Why, no," answered the Storyteller, feeling embarrassed. Now he took a closer look at the lady and saw how lovely she was. "I really don't know how I could have overlooked you. You are really quite beautiful."

Now it was the woman's turn to be embarrassed. Her cheeks became nearly the same color as her red hair. "Well, shouldn't you get your apple and continue whatever you were doing?"

"But of course," said the man as he picked an apple from one of the boughs that hung over the woman's head. Then, suddenly, he sat down next to her.

"What are you doing?" she demanded.

"I'm continuing what I was doing, which is enjoying the beautiful scenery," replied the Storyteller, flashing her a smile.

"Oh," said the woman, trying not to show her amusement.

After this awkward beginning, the two began to talk. The man told the woman all about himself, including, of course, his storytelling. As he spoke, he was surprised at how easy it was to express himself. Although he was a marvelous storyteller, he had always had great difficulty in speaking simply and directly about his own thoughts and feelings. How wonderful it was to talk this way!

So, dear Reader, several hours passed. Finally, the woman turned to the man and said, "I have enjoyed hearing your story, but now I must leave." With these words, the woman vanished.

The Storyteller called out, "Wait! Come back! Where did you go?" Sadly, he realized that he had been doing all the talking and so knew nothing about the woman. He cried out a second time, "I want to hear your story!"

A faint, faraway voice answered, "My tale is too sad to tell. Goodbye and good luck in your storytelling." The grove was now silent.

The man picked another apple from the tree and, sitting down, began to wonder about the woman. Where had she gone? Was her story really so sad?

Several weeks passed. The man continued to tell his tales, but now all of his stories were about the woman he had met in the apple grove. People began to notice this. One of them asked, "Who is this woman you are always talking about? Is she real?"

"I don't know," answered the Storyteller. "She disappeared before I could find out anything about her." He paused. "But she must be real. There is no way I could have dreamed up such a lovely creature."

Then, the Storyteller did something he had never done. He left the people right in the middle of one of his stories. He had decided that he must find the woman and he must hear her tale. He returned to the same apple grove where he had met her and waited. Many days passed, but the lady did not appear.

However, after many more days of waiting, the Storyteller's patience was finally rewarded. As he sat, leaning against one of the apple trees in the very same spot he had shared with the woman, she suddenly appeared, standing before him.

"Hello," said the Storyteller. "How are you doing today?"

"Oh, I am the same as yesterday," she replied.

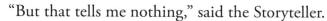

"But that tells me nothing," said the Storyteller.

"I know," answered the woman.

The Storyteller held fast to the question he wanted to ask. "Please sit down and join me for a while. I have waited for such a long time." The woman smiled at him and then sat down beside him. He continued, "What is your story?"

The woman's eyes became clouded as she lowered her head. "I cannot tell you. It is too sad. It will only fill you with melancholy."

But the Storyteller persisted. "I really must hear your story. Since I am the Storyteller, I can understand and appreciate even the saddest of tales. Please tell me. You must trust me on this."

After a long while of just sitting and gazing into the Storyteller's eyes, the woman finally agreed to tell her story. As she began, the Storyteller was shocked at the misery and tragedy that had filled the woman's life. All that she had loved had been taken from her. Her husband and her only child had been destroyed by an evil wizard, and her home had been taken away by a tax lord.

She had become so desolate that she had wished to disappear from the earth and she had gotten her wish. Only occasionally did she reappear for brief moments in this apple grove.

The Storyteller was deeply saddened by the woman's story. He put her hands in his and said, "You have lost many precious things in your life, but you still possess the most important thing of all. You have yourself. You possess a spirit that radiates warmth and understanding. Thank goodness all of the tragedy of your life has not destroyed this! You are the only person to whom I have ever been able to speak so freely about myself. This is something at which I marvel."

The woman smiled at the man, touched by his words. Sensing her thoughts, the Storyteller put his arms around her. Gently, he gave her a kiss that expressed compassion. Then he gave her a kiss that expressed something more. With this, both felt the sweetness of a new love.

After more embraces and more kisses, the Storyteller looked deeply into the woman's eyes and said, "Let me tell you how your story will end. You will be dearly loved by a new husband. He will give you great happiness. Together you will have children, and together you will explore the world. No more tragedy will touch your life, and I am certain that you will never again want to disappear. In short, your story will have a happy ending."

With these words, the Storyteller stood up. Reaching down, he pulled the woman up to his side. They looked lovingly at each other, and then, arm in arm, they left the apple grove.

The End

"'Sir, I have no dragons, but I do have a freshly baked strawberry pie.'"

The Dragon Slayer

Once there was a knight who had no friends. He was so busy slaying dragons that he had never taken the time to stop and get to know any of the folk in the surrounding castles. All that the people knew of him was that he was very good at slaying large, frightening beasts.

One day the knight went out looking for yet another dragon to slay, but there seemed to be no dragons about. He decided to stop at a little cottage and inquire if any dragons had been sighted. The man got off his horse and walked over to the cottage door, which was slightly ajar. He could smell something delicious coming from within. Also, he heard someone humming a bright little tune.

"Hark!" he said in his most courtly manner. "Is there someone within who would know the whereabouts of a dragon?"

After a few moments, the cottage door was opened wide and a beautiful young woman stood before him. She smiled and said, "Sir, I have no dragons, but I do have a freshly baked strawberry pie. You are most welcome to come in and partake of a piece."

The man was startled by the invitation. All he could manage to say was, "But I have never tasted strawberry pie before."

Undaunted, the young woman quickly replied, "How will you know if you like it if you never try it?"

"You are certainly right," answered the dragon slayer. And with that, he strode into the cottage.

The woman motioned for him to warm himself near the fireplace. Then she poured him a mug of fresh spring water and cut him a slice of the strawberry pie. At first the man ate very slowly, and then, as he discovered how much he liked the pie, he ate more quickly and with great relish. Seeing this, the woman smiled and cut him another piece.

The man exclaimed, "This pie was made by an angel! It is the best I have ever tasted!" Now he found himself smiling and wanting to learn more about the lady. The two began to talk, exchanging many pleasantries. What was most strange was that the knight forgot all about dragons. He was completely captivated by the woman.

Days passed, then weeks, and the man was still at the cottage, spending many happy hours in the company of the woman. He found great pleasure in mending her cottage roof, tending her garden, and—what was most unexpected for a dragon slayer—washing her cups and dishes. This made the woman very happy. She began to think that the dragon slayer would stay with her forever.

Sadly, dear Reader, there came a time when the knight remembered his dragon-slaying days. He became very downcast, recalling the thrill and excitement of slaying huge and dangerous creatures.

He turned to the woman and said, "You are very beautiful and I love you, but I can no longer stay with you. I must do what I have always done. I must seek and destroy dragons."

The woman began to cry. She could not believe that the man would leave her to continue such a frightening and lonely task as slaying dragons, but she saw that she could do nothing to make him stay.

She asked, "Will you ever come again?"

"I cannot say," answered the once-again dragon slayer. With these parting words and a kiss, the man left the woman.

Many years passed, and the dragon slayer traveled far and wide, slaying many dragons. He became famous for his great skill and daring. People even sang songs about him.

One day his thoughts returned to the woman whom he had met so long ago. He remembered her beauty and, most of all, he remembered the love she had given him. With this, he put down his dragon-slaying lance, mounted his horse, and rode in great haste back to the woman's cottage.

"Will she still be there?" he wondered. "And, will she still love me?"

At last the dragon slayer came to the woman's cottage. He was overjoyed to see it. The door was slightly ajar. Happily, he remembered that it had been just the same the first time he had met the lady. He got off his horse and quickly rushed up to the door. After a moment of hesitation, he entered the cottage.

All was changed. There was no smell of strawberry pie, no warm fire in the fireplace, and, worst of all, no beautiful woman. The cottage was deserted. It looked as if it had not been used for a long time.

The man sat down near the fireplace. Great sadness fell upon him. How could the woman not be here? How could she leave him so totally alone? But then he realized that he had done the same to her.

As he thought of this, he noticed what appeared to be an envelope nailed to the mantel over the fireplace. He took it down and looked inside. Carefully, he pulled out a letter. It was from the woman! It read:

"To my love,

I do not know if you will ever read this. But if you do, I want you to remember that I will always love you."

As he finished reading the last words, the letter crumbled in his hands and fell to the floor. It must have been written many years ago. The man cried. He realized how much he truly loved her. If only he had known this a long time ago.

With great sadness, the man left the cottage and spent the rest of his days looking for the woman. He never slew another dragon.

The End

"Sitting down on a stool, she put her flute to her lips and began to play a tune."

The Duet of Love

The woman sat in a dark room. She was trying to hide from her sad thoughts. She had lost at love for the second time. She wondered if she would ever again reach out to another person. Would she be willing to step up to the precipice and plunge, head over heels, into the arms of another?

Well, there was no time to think about it now. She shook off her gloom and, gathering herself together, started out of her little house on her way to the town square. Today was her turn to play her flute. Everyone in the village took turns in providing entertainment, always at the noon hour. All the people would gather together, coming out of their homes and pausing in their daily pursuits to watch and listen to whatever was offered by their neighbors. It was the way of the town to share in the making of art, in all its various forms. Some played instruments like the woman, and others painted pictures or carved figures.

The woman hurried to the square. Sitting down on a stool, she put her flute to her lips and began to play a tune. The people gathered round, and as they listened, they nodded their heads in agreement that this was a very sweet melody.

"Ah! But it is such a sad little tune," they thought. As the woman continued to play the flute, something magical began to happen. The woman's tune began to rise into the air. It traveled far and wide, reaching out to many of the inhabitants for miles around, even traveling across the great sea that could only be seen from the mountaintops. It was in search of a person who would understand the meaning of the woman's music, someone who would respond to its call.

Dear Reader, it so happened that on the other side of the sea there was a young man, who had also had his share of heartache. Sitting in his hut, he poured out his heart in words he scribbled onto a scrap of paper. As he wrote, the woman's tune hovered over his small home. It lingered there and then drifted inside, repeating over and over again its musical refrain. The man stopped what he was doing and listened. He could hear the beat of a kindred spirit. Picking up his pen, he began to write with renewed vigor. His words now matched the notes of the woman's music.

Together, a song formed. The words blended with the music, almost like they had always been as one. United, they lifted into the air and floated back over the great sea, over the mountaintops, and into the ear of the woman who was still playing her flute.

She was enchanted by the man's words. Gradually, she began to sense that these musings might be the response that she so dearly longed for—the beginning of a new love. She played her flute with passion, responding to the words the man had written. The townspeople began to notice the change in the woman's face and in her playing. Where she had looked so sad, she now appeared hopeful and even radiant. Her music had also changed, now becoming quite cheerful with ascending runs and trills. All the men, women, and children prayed for her, hoping this change would continue. Would her tune be able to bring her the dream that she had always had in her heart? Everyone continued to pray as the woman played on.

Though so far away, the man could clearly hear the woman's tune. He now knew that he must follow it, wherever it led him. Packing up his belongings, he began what became a long journey. He traveled on foot, then by boat over the sea, and then climbed over the great mountaintops. Always, he could hear the woman's music.

She continued to play her flute for days and days, not stopping for food or drink. Then, early one morning, the man walked up to her and asked, "Do you believe in love?" She put down her flute and replied, "Yes, I do."

With this, the man sang to her, "I heard your tune from across the sea. It found my heart and made it beat. Oh, won't you come and marry me?"

"I will," answered the woman. And so the two spent the rest of their lives making many happy songs together, with music from the woman and words from the man. It became, as you may have already guessed, a duet of love that lasted forever and ever.

The End

"Once there was a family of foxes."

The Liar Family

Once there was a family of foxes. There was Father Fox, Mother Fox, Brother Fox, Sister Fox, and newly born Baby Fox. They lived in a comfortable den hidden in the hills. Everyone in the animal world knew them as the Liar Family. In short order, dear Reader, you will learn how they got their name.

"Now remember," Father Fox instructed his family, "the bigger the lie, the better the lie. And think about this: If anyone is so foolish as to believe us, don't they deserve the consequence?"

All of the foxes nodded in agreement with the words of the older fox. Lying was a long tradition in their family and was not to be questioned.

"Now, Mother Fox. I know you must stay home with Baby Fox, but Brother and Sister Fox need to come along with me. We must go out and collect our dinner through the use of cunning and deceit. Time to be off!"

Out of their secret den crept the three foxes early on a cold morning. They were in search of some ill-gotten gain. The more trickery involved, the better.

Back in the den, little Baby Fox smiled up at his mother and said his first words. "Mother Fox, what beautiful teeth you have!"

"All the better to tear into a fat little rabbit!" his mother replied. Baby Fox was horrified thinking about a cute little bunny. He was confused by his mother's words. Not knowing what else to do, he nodded off to sleep. Meanwhile, the three other foxes were on the prowl to lick clean an unsuspecting farmer's barnyard.

"See that plump chicken over there?" asked Father Fox. "Go trick her into coming with us, Brother Fox." So Brother Fox went over to the chicken and began a series of lies that his father had carefully taught him.

"Come with us, dear chicken. Your master, the farmer, wants you to stroll with us and gather pretty flowers for his lady's table. You will make him so happy by presenting him with a colorful nosegay. Come! A patch of flowers is just within an easy walk."

"Oh, thank you, Mr. Fox. Thank you for your helpful hint. I will go immediately. Which way are the flowers?" asked the chicken.

"Oh, you need only to follow me, my sister, and our father. Come away with us. It will take just a few moments to reach the flowers, and then you will be overwhelmed by their bountifulness and splendor. Think how happy all will be!"

So, the unsuspecting chicken was fooled by the lies of Brother Fox. Father Fox smiled in approval. It only took a short walk and then—snap! Brother Fox quickly broke the neck of the poor chicken.

The three foxes continued on their way. By the end of the morning, they had collected a whole host of unsuspecting creatures. There was, as you already know, a chicken, and now they had a rabbit and two squirrels. All had been acquired through the use of some very convincing lies. The three foxes smiled at each other, laughing with delight and singing:

"We are foxes
and lies are our game!
Merrily we hunt
for our ill-gotten gain!"

Satisfied with their morning hunt, the three returned to their secret den. Father Fox entered first, followed by Brother Fox and then Sister Fox.

"How did it go today, Father Fox?" asked Mother Fox.

"Oh, it was such a wonderful time! It is amazing how gullible the animals are that we seek!" said Father Fox. "One lie, maybe two, and then they are ours. I almost wish it wasn't so easy." With this, Father Fox held up all the animals they had captured.

Just then Baby Fox woke up and saw the limp bodies of the chicken, rabbit, and two squirrels. He exclaimed as loudly as a baby fox could, "Oh, no! What has happened to these poor creatures, dear Father?"

"Why, I, your brother, and sister simply told them a lie, and they came willingly into our trap," said Father Fox.

"That doesn't sound fair!" replied Baby Fox.

"Fair? Why do we have to be fair? Remember, Baby Fox: the bigger the lie, the better the lie," roared Father Fox. "It is our family motto and don't you forget it!"

With that retort, Father Fox hit Baby Fox on his nose, causing him to cry out in pain. Baby Fox turned to Mother Fox, but she looked at him with disgust and she, too, gave him a whack on the nose.

Again, Baby Fox cried out, repeating his words, "This isn't fair!" Leaving his mother's arms, he crawled farther into his family's den and, not knowing what else to do, he fell asleep.

While he slept, the other four foxes—Father Fox, Mother Fox, Brother Fox, and Sister Fox—talked about what a terrible fox Baby Fox was for daring to question their behavior. They had always lied. Why should they stop now? It had helped them fool a whole lot of stupid animals into becoming the foxes' dinner. The more they talked, the angrier they became about Baby Fox. Insults spewed out of their mouths as they tore apart the character of the little fox. Finally, they could stand it no longer. They decided they must deal with the little fox who worried about fairness and telling the truth.

"Let us leave Baby Fox all alone," said Mother Fox. "That way we will teach him a lesson!"

"Yes!" agreed Brother and Sister Fox. "We can leave him a note that is full of lies, saying that we will come back."

"But we won't," said Father Fox.

"Yes!" they all shouted together with glee.

So Mother Fox wrote a note to Baby Fox that read, "Do not worry. Your family loves you dearly. Just stay in the den and we will be back soon."

Mother Fox then turned to her fellow conspirators and said, "Since our Baby Fox is such a trusting little fox, he will believe us and do just as we say. Without our return, he will become very hungry and probably die! Let's go quickly now so all can be done!"

And so, without delay, the four foxes gathered up their belongings and left their den without another word.

The little fox slept and slept, dreaming of his mother and father and his brother and sister and how much he loved them. Eventually, he roused from his slumber.

"Mother Fox! Mother Fox! Where are you?" Baby Fox cried out. He rubbed his eyes and looked all around. Everywhere he looked, he saw no hint of his family. Then lo! Thank goodness! There was a piece of paper on the floor of the den. It was from his mother! Not to worry. They would all be returning for him.

Sadly, dear Reader, you and I know the truth. Baby Fox's family did not love him. Full of trust, Baby Fox followed his mother's directions and waited several days for his family to return.

Not a stupid fox by any means, Baby Fox eventually realized that if he didn't do something soon, he would surely die of hunger. Gathering up all his remaining strength, he crawled out of the den. It was very dark. He could barely see where to go. Carefully, he crept down a hill and into a large, even darker forest. Only a bit of the moon lit the way. His stomach gnawed at him, telling him he would soon be dead if he didn't get something to eat. Then his little legs collapsed and he fell to the ground. Looking up at the sky, he sobbed until his little fox eyes were red and swollen.

"Why has my family left me all alone?" he cried out.

Suddenly, he heard a swoosh of fluttering wings above his head and the words, "Whooo are yooou?" It was an owl. The owl made another pass over the fox, and again he called out, "Whooo are yooou?"

The little fox whimpered in a faint little voice, "I am Baby Fox and am very near to death!"

The owl was a friendly sort, but also, of course, a very wise creature, as owls often are. He wanted to help the little fox, but he knew that foxes could be very cunning. Perhaps this was a trick, a cruel lie that would entice the owl to become dinner for the fox. The owl circled overhead a third time. Then his basic goodness of character would have it no other way. He swooped down and gently grabbed the little fox by the nape of his neck. High up into the tops of the trees he flew with the little fox held firmly in his talons.

He took the baby fox to his family's home. There, the owl's wife nursed the little fox back to health. Eventually, the fox grew up, and like many owls he became a great scholar. Although he didn't look like his fellow colleagues, the fox became well respected for his wisdom and great appreciation for fair play. Throughout his life, he always told the truth in all of his dealings with the other animals. His motto was, "The greater the truth, the better the truth!"

The End

"While she slept, creatures gathered along the edge of the meadow."

The Love Child

Once there was a woman who loved a man. He was the stars, the flowers, and all that filled her life with happiness. What was even more wonderful was that he loved her too.

Although the village had not blessed them, the two lived together. They lived in a little cabin deep in a forest. Every day the man would go out to cut wood to sell in the village. With the money from the wood, he was able to buy everything that the woman and he needed to live.

However, he often complained that he did not like having to go to the village to sell the wood. The village people always asked him the same questions. "When are you and the woman going to be blessed to live as one? What if she should have a child? Without a blessing, whose child would it be?" The man often became angry with these questions. More than once, he had fought with some of the villagers.

One day the woman told the man that she had some important questions for him. Putting down his ax, he turned to listen. First she asked, "When will we be blessed to live as one?" Then she asked, "What would you do if I was with child?" This was followed by, "Without a blessing, whose child would it be?"

The man became angry. He took up his ax and flung it into the side of the cabin. "Why do you ask me such questions?" he demanded.

The woman became quiet and then spoke, "Because I am with child."

The man sat down and put his head in his hands. He said, "I love you very much, but I cannot be blessed to live with you as one. I do not believe in the blessing. It has no meaning for me."

The woman began to sob. The man felt her hurt and tried to comfort her, but it was to no avail. She cried out, "Whose child will it be?"

The man became frustrated and angry. He stood up and said, "Not mine!" With these words, the man took his ax and left. He never returned.

Time passed. The woman had the child. She was a beautiful baby girl. Since the woman and man had not been blessed to live as one, the child was without her father's namesake. In the village, she was simply known as "the love child." Despite this, the woman loved the child very much and did the best she could to raise the girl. However, after nine years of a hard life, the woman died, leaving the love child all alone.

With the woman's death, the child went to the village. She asked each villager, "Whose child am I?"

Each of them answered her back with the same reply. "You are no one's child. You are a love child."

This, of course, made the child sad and frightened, but she continued to seek out people and ask them the same question. She felt that she must belong to someone. Thus began the love child's travels. Everywhere she went, she asked, "Whose child am I?" Sadly, no one claimed her, but she continued on.

Eventually, the child came to a great forest. At the edge of the trees stood a large sign. It read: "Do not enter! This forest is ruled by huge monsters who will eat you!" The child was frightened by the sign, but if she were to continue her search, she had to pass through the forest. She entered it with much trepidation, but also with great determination.

As she walked along, she found the forest very quiet. There was no sound of a living thing. How strange it all seemed to her. After walking many hours, the love child looked around for a place to rest. Suddenly, a beautiful meadow magically appeared. The love child smiled and immediately laid down upon the soft grass. In a wink, she found herself surrounded by a colorful ring of flowers. "Oh!" she said. "How lovely! I have never seen such a pretty place to nap." In no time at all, the little girl was fast asleep.

While she slept, creatures gathered along the edge of the meadow. They were very large with black, stringy hair and long, protruding teeth. One of them roared, "Ho! Ho! Look what we have caught for dinner!"

With this the little girl woke with a start. Seeing the ugly monsters, she tried to run away, but the flower ring held her fast. She cried out, "Oh, please do not eat me! My life has been so short and so forlorn. Please let me live to find at least a moment of happiness!"

The smallest monster had been studying the love child carefully, and now he spoke up, saying, "Let's hear the little girl's story, and if it is as sad as she says, maybe we should spare her." Since all of the monsters liked hearing stories very much, they agreed to the plan. The love child began to tell her tale. As she described the sadness of losing a father, a mother, and not belonging to anyone, the monsters began to cry. The little girl had touched even their mean hearts.

"Okay. You can go, little one. We surely hope you will find some happiness," said the largest of the beasts as he wiped his eyes.

The love child thanked the monsters for their mercy and once again continued on her journey, looking for an answer to her question. She walked a long way, going even deeper into the forest. Just as it was getting dark, she came to a clearing. There stood a large cabin. Tired and hungry, she decided to knock on the cabin door and see if someone might give her some bread and water. She walked up to the door and knocked. After awhile, she heard heavy footsteps coming from within the cabin. The door was opened and there stood a man. He looked at her with stern eyes and asked, "Who are you? And what are you doing in a forest full of monsters? Don't you know that they might eat you?"

The girl nodded to the man and said in a very small voice, "I am no one's child. I am a love child."

With these words, the man suddenly changed his demeanor and said to her, "Come in. I will give you food and a place to rest." The child entered the cabin. Quickly, he gave her some water and then some bread and cheese. Then he motioned for her to rest on a nearby cot. As the child closed her eyes, she found herself slipping into a deep sleep, one filled with strange dreams of a man and a woman living in a cabin deep in a forest.

When the child awoke the next day, she was surprised to see the man looking at her as he sat in a nearby chair. She wondered how long he had been doing this.

The man asked her, "Where do you come from?"

The girl replied, "I used to live in a cabin deep in a forest with a woman, but . . . she died."

The man looked at the sad eyes of the child. He asked, "So why did you pass through such a dangerous place as these woods?"

She lowered her head and said, "I must travel through these woods so that I can continue to ask my question."

The man was puzzled and asked, "What question?"

The child looked up at him and answered, "I ask the question, 'Whose child am I?'"

With these words, the man put his head in his hands and said, "Words out of my past." Then he looked at the child and said, "I never thought I would ever hear those words again." He paused for a long while. "You look and sound just like the woman. You were her child, and . . . you are my child."

The child's eyes opened wide. Had she finally found whose child she was? Before the child could think or do anything more, the man put his arms around her. He held her close and told her over and over again that she was his child. He had not been able to say these words years ago, but now he could.

"You are my child. I love you. I loved the woman, your mother. Please forgive me for leaving both of you. My anger got the better of me."

The child kissed the man. Softly, she said, "I forgive you."

From that day on, the two shared a happy life. So, dear Reader, the child grew up and became a lovely woman. She was still always referred to as the love child, but never again did she have to ask, "Whose child am I?"

The End

"All that he cared about was a pile of gold..."

The Hermit

Once there was a hermit who lived in a large hole deep in the hills of a small village. He had once lived in the town as an ordinary man, but his jealousy of others had brought him to his present state. All that he cared about was a pile of gold that he had stolen, coin by coin, from the people.

If someone happened by his hole, the hermit would say, "Can you please help me, kind sir? I am old and feeble and need help to get out of this great pit."

The unsuspecting person would say, "I will help you!" After pulling the hermit out of the hole, this helpful person would then be hit hard on the head by this very same hermit. As the hapless person lay unconscious on the ground, the hermit would quickly search his pockets for gold. After that, he would scramble back into his hole and wait for his next victim to come by.

This rogue's ruse worked quite well for many years. Always, the person targeted by the hermit would feel sorry for him. Then—bang! He would be hit on his head and made lighter of his coins.

As more and more people came to learn firsthand of the hermit's treachery, a general alarm was finally put out in the village. "Steer clear of the hermit! He is not to be trusted!"

Meanwhile, the hermit sat quietly on his great pile of golden coins. Because the pile had become so large, he was now forced to sit outside on top of it. The gold took up all the room in his hole, so he could no longer enjoy the comforts it had once provided him. But he didn't care because his only concern was in protecting his pile of gold. "I can manage even in bad weather," he said to himself. "My gold is my most precious possession. It must be protected at all costs!"

One day it began to rain. At first the drops were small ones. "No problem," said the hermit. "I can easily manage this bit of dampness." Muttering, he covered his head with a hat.

Drip, drip, drip!

The raindrops continued to fall. The hermit began to sniffle as he struggled to keep dry.

Drip, drip, drip!

The drips now became splashes.

Splash, splash, splash!

The hermit, being quite old, began to weaken under what now became a downpour. His sniffles became coughs.

"Cough, cough, cough!"

He was now totally drenched and totally miserable.

"Well, I guess I better get into my hole and find a dry spot to wait out this storm," he grumbled. However, try as he might, he could find no room to squeeze through the pile of coins. The gold coins were heavy and in great numbers. Every time he tried to move a few to the side, others would slide in the way, making it quite impossible for the hermit to gain entrance to his hole. The many gold coins crowded him out. Exhausted in his efforts to enter his hole, he cried out, "I am an old hermit who needs help. Help, help!"

A young man was hurrying home after a day of hunting in the hills. He heard the cries of the hermit, but he also heard in his head the warning, "Beware of the hermit! He will only hit you on the head and take your gold! His cries are all lies!" The young man heeded the words of the villagers, and so he headed home directly.

The hermit sputtered out one cough after another as the rain pelted down on his head. He continued to try to dig his way into his hole, but, alas, the coins were too numerous and too heavy. He could have left his gold and sought a dry spot elsewhere, but no. He would not leave his gold. It was his most precious possession. So, he continued to sit on top of the great golden pile.

Splash, splash, splash!

"Cough, cough, cough!"

He yelled out his worst expletive. "Dingelsplat the weather! Dingelsplat the people! I hate everyone and everything!" Still, he would not leave his gold. Finally, he let out his last great volley of coughs. His whole body shook, and then he was silent. In the end, he lay dead on top of his great pile of gold.

Dear Reader, you may ask, "What happened to the hermit's great wealth?" Well, Mother Nature stepped in to cover the hermit, his gold, and his hole. She directed the North Wind to blow a great quantity of leaves and dirt over the remains of the hermit and all that he had possessed. In the end, it was as if the hermit, his gold, and the hole had never been.

The End

"...he decided he must pursue her, and he did through the dance."

The Dance of Love

The woman lived in a town where all the important moments of life were celebrated in dance. There was a dance to express the joy of a birth, one to show appreciation for a friend, one to give respect for another's work, and one to bless the harvesting of a crop. Among the many dances, the most important one was the dance of love. This dance marked the meeting of a man and a woman and the beginning of their life together. Whoever danced this dance made a vow to his or her partner to fulfill its promise. The couple dancing this dance would love each other forever.

One morning the woman rose from her bed to begin preparations for the dance that everyone in the village would be doing that evening. This particular dance was done once a year, and it celebrated the spirit of the town and the feeling of camaraderie among the villagers.

The woman smiled to herself. This dance meant that she would be seeing people whom she hadn't seen for a while. Everyone would be there. She hurried to get ready. When all was done, she left to join the festivities.

This annual event was always held outside in the middle of the town. Members of the village provided flute and harp music for the dancing. A large fire was always lit to give the people light and warmth. Through the years, the fire had come to signify the spirit of the town. The bright flames matched the bright spirits of the dancing people.

The woman greeted several of her fellow villagers as she joined the large circle dancing around the fire. Everyone responded to her with the same warm greeting. Happiness and joy filled her as she moved with them. It was such a comfort to belong to such a wonderful community. She loved to dance. It was so natural and wonderful to express her feelings in this manner. Everyone around her felt the same. It was the way of the town.

While everyone was dancing to the joyful tunes of the village musicians, a tall, dark-haired man suddenly walked into view. The woman could see by the flicker of the firelight that this man was a stranger. As she studied his face, she could also see that the man wanted to join the dancers, but he seemed unsure how to accomplish this. The woman decided to help him.

As the circle moved her closer to him, she dropped the hand of the dancer next to her and extended hers to him. Delighted, he quickly took her hand and joined the circle. Then he turned to her and gave her a look that startled her. It was a very deep and penetrating one. The man's eyes seemed to have a magical quality. The woman quickly glanced away.

The music played and the dancers danced on. Every time the woman peered over at the man, she found him looking back at her. Again and again she had to turn away. She could not hold his gaze. His eyes were more intense than any she had ever seen.

As the music paused for a moment, the man turned to the woman and told her that he was from a faraway land called New Yonderlay. He had been sent to study the ways of the woman's village. His people wanted to learn about her people.

Hearing this, the woman told the man that all he needed to do was to dance with them. With this, she took him by the hand and showed him the dance that expressed friendship. The movements were happy ones, filled with lively skips and the waving of arms. The man found himself now smiling at his new friend.

Later, the man joined the other villagers to dance in a celebration of the town's spirit. For the first time in his life, the man felt a real sense of belonging. This was something the people of New Yonderlay did not have. The music played on and the dancers continued to dance. Everywhere, faces were happy.

As the evening progressed, the man was drawn again and again to the woman. Her high spirits and beauty fascinated him. And so, dear Reader, he decided he must pursue her, and he did through the dance.

The villagers began to notice the man's interest in the woman. They smiled to one another. Then they signaled for the musicians to play another tune. It was announced that the next dance would be the dance of love.

Hearing this, the man took the woman's arm and started to lead her out to the dancing area. The woman stopped him and told him that only lovers could dance this dance. She tried to explain more of the dance's significance to the man, but he looked at her with those same penetrating eyes and then, without further hesitation, led her out to do the dance. His eyes continued to play a kind of magic on her. She was completely captivated.

All of the villagers stepped back and watched the man and the woman dance. Their movements were at first very lively, matching the music that was played. Together they moved quickly around the fire with many turns and flourishes. Then the music changed to a slow melody. The movements of the man and woman now changed with the music. They held each other very close and now moved as one. Each was caught up in a great feeling of love. The dance continued for a long time.

When the man and the woman reached the highest level of emotion, the dance ended. Then all of the villagers joined hands and formed a large circle around the couple as they stood quietly together, looking into each other's eyes. After a few moments, the circle parted, and the man and the woman walked off together.

When they had left the fire, the dancers, and the musicians far behind, the woman turned to the man and asked him if he understood the meaning of the dance that they had done. He said that he did and, taking the woman into his arms, he gave her a kiss that expressed love. The woman was swept away by his passion, and so the man and woman loved each other throughout the night.

Many weeks passed, and the man and the woman lived together in great joy. All the promise of the dance was fulfilled. The man and the woman had never been happier.

But one day the man felt something was missing or incomplete. He remembered his own people. He remembered the people of New Yonderlay. Ultimately, he came to believe that he must complete his mission for them. He must bring them what he had learned about the village and its dancing.

When he told the woman this, she could not believe his words. She loved him, and she knew that he loved her. Why would he want to leave their home? But the man told the woman that it was her home, not his. He must keep his promise to the people of New Yonderlay. With these words, the man left the woman.

Many days passed. The woman spent her time avoiding her fellow villagers. She stayed away from the dances of the town.

Meanwhile, the man returned to his home. He told his people of the village. He told them of the dancing and of its special meaning. He told them how the dances could bring great joy and love to New Yonderlay.

At first his people listened with interest, but as time passed, they eventually forgot what the man had told them about the village. Tragically, they continued their lives as they had always done, without great caring or love. As more time passed, even the man forgot about the village. He forgot about the wonderful feelings that he had felt dancing with the villagers, and even about the love he had felt for the woman. He forgot all that he had learned.

Back at the village, the woman wept for a long time. Her grief brought her down to the lowest level of despair. She could not believe that the man had forgotten her and their love together. They had danced the dance of love. They had made a commitment to love each other forever. How was anything else possible after dancing the dance of love?

The other villagers began to notice the absence of the woman. They became alarmed. All assembled at the town center and then moved in a worried dance to the woman's cottage.

Once they got there, they called for the woman to come out. After a long while, the woman finally joined her fellow villagers. When they saw the grief on her face and learned the cause for it, they took her into their arms and told her that she must now dance the dance of healing. They would help her through this dance to be happy again. So, with great caring, the villagers helped to lessen the woman's pain. They helped her through the slow and caring movements of the dance, at first carrying her, and then later encouraging her to find her own footing.

When they left, the woman felt she had finally overcome her grief. She was able to smile. Then, she realized that someday she would again be able to dance the dance of love.

The End

"'...make time for those who wish you well.'"

The Clock

The young woman searched the face of her stepmother. She was looking for a trace of kindness, some shred of love.

Her stepmother said, "Now that your father is dead, you need to be on your way!"

"But you have a great home with many rooms that Father has provided you. I take up only a very small space. Put me anywhere! I will cheerfully remain, even in the smallest corner!" the stepdaughter pleaded.

"No. It is now time for you to go," the stepmother said coldly.

Her stepdaughter persisted. "But why are my stepbrother and stepsister allowed to stay and not me? Haven't I always been there for you, especially when Father died? Didn't I comfort you? Where were they?"

Her stepmother became very angry and shouted back, "You ask too many questions. How dare you question me on anything!"

For a long time now, this mother had been jealous of her stepdaughter. This daughter had become more beautiful each day, and each day her stepmother's hatred had only increased. With her husband gone, she was not going to tolerate this anymore.

The daughter's stepbrother now appeared. "Get rid of her!" screamed the stepmother. Following his mother's order, he grabbed his unwanted sister and dragged her to the back door. With one mighty toss, he threw her out of the house.

Then the other sister appeared. Hearing her stepsister's cries, she exclaimed, "What a bother she is!" She, like her mother, was also very jealous of this extra family member. "Why did she have to be so beautiful? Why did she have to be so sweet?" Realizing that this sister was now finally on the way out, she rejoiced, "Now I will have all of Stepfather's jewels!" Seeing her mother was within earshot, she quickly added, "Once you are dead, of course, dear Mother!" Waving farewell, this sister shouted, "Goodbye, Stepsister, and may you never return! We wish you all the worst!"

Her brother smiled in agreement. "Come, my dear and only sister of mine. Let's help our mother count her gold! I can't think of a more pleasant task! Let's go unlock her treasure vault and start counting immediately!" Off they went.

The exiled sister was now outside the warmth of her stepmother's great house. Sadly, dear Reader, I don't refer to the warmth of a loving home. Oh, no! Only the stove gave out any kind of warmth. The cheerfulness of earlier days had long ago disappeared when the girl's father had died. The rejected daughter sat on the ground. She ached, remembering those long-ago days when her father and real mother had been alive. Now she was without a family or a home. She was all alone.

By chance, the young woman had been thrown on top of a garbage heap just outside the back door of her stepmother's large mansion. All sorts of unwanted items were stacked on this pile, including the now-discarded daughter. She stood up and dusted off her clothes. They were covered with bits and pieces from the trash heap. Sadly, she knew she must now be on her way.

Before she started, she turned around and gave one last look at what she had once called home. Her eyes caught the top of an old clock sticking out of the garbage heap. She remembered how its ticking and chiming had given her so much pleasure in earlier days. It seemed to look at her unhappily, now that it was unable to tick or to ring out with its sweet chimes. Just like her, the clock seemed forlorn and downcast.

The woman decided to take the old clock with her. After all, it had been thrown away. The family no longer wanted it. She leaned down and carefully brushed away the garbage that surrounded it. Wrapping it in a rag, she started on her way.

Luckily for the woman, she had friends who would help her. They didn't possess much in terms of wealth, but they shared what they had. They gave her a small, run-down cottage, a little bed, and a wobbly table and chair. After going from shop to shop in the nearby village, she also obtained a job working as a seamstress. With this she was able to live, although very modestly.

After several weeks, she was finally able to save some coins from her wages. She planned to make repairs on her little home. Many things needed to be fixed. The roof leaked; a window was broken. The list of repairs was a long one.

Then she remembered the old family clock that she had saved from her stepmother's garbage heap. It came to her that she must repair the clock first before anything else. Again, she covered the clock with a rag and took it to the clockmaker in the nearby village. She walked quickly but carefully.

Finally, she arrived at his workshop. As she entered, she heard the ticking of many clocks. It was almost twelve o'clock. As if in a greeting, all the clocks began to chime the hour.

"How wonderful!" the woman exclaimed. "If only my clock could sing out, too!"

The woman walked up to the clockmaker, with her clock under her arm. Carefully, she unwrapped the clock and set it on the counter.

"Sir, can you fix my clock? I know it is old, but it is the only thing that I have from my family. I have saved this amount of coins. Is it enough?" As she spoke, she showed him the small number of coins in her hand.

The clockmaker looked at the old clock and then at the young woman. Shaking his head, he said, "It appears that you both have suffered, but being only a clockmaker, all I can do is to fix your clock." Looking at the few coins, the clockmaker said, "This is just the right amount to pay for my services. Come back tomorrow and all will be done." The woman was so happy that she danced around the shop with great joy and even gave the clockmaker a kiss.

"See you tomorrow!" she cried out as she skipped all the way back to her cottage. All that night she dreamed about the clock that would be coming back to life.

The next day, bright and early, she was back at the shop of the clockmaker. "Is my clock ticking and is it chiming, too?"

"Not yet. But soon it will be! All you have to do is to take it home and wind it with this key." With these words, the clockmaker handed the woman a golden key. "If you take good care of the clock, then it will take good care of you."

Hurriedly, but carefully, the woman took the clock back to her cottage. She had already decided where she would put it. She placed the clock on her one small table near her bed. Taking out the key, she began to wind it. First, she wound the chimes and then, the clock itself. The clock began to tick, but then it did something else. It said, "Thank you!"

"What?" asked the woman, looking all around her small cottage.

Again, she heard, "Thank you!" The clock had actually talked! Thus began a very interesting conversation between the woman and the clock. The clock explained to her that many years ago her father had done a great favor for the neighborhood fairy. This fairy was no ordinary fairy, but a fairy of great importance, possessing many magical powers.

For his help, the fairy had granted her father a wish. Always poking fun, her father had said, "Well, why don't you make my clock talk?" In a flash, the fairy had sprinkled fairy dust on the clock and, as requested, it had begun to talk.

Before she left, the fairy had given her father specific instructions about the care of this now special clock. First, he must keep the clock wound. If the clock wound down, then it would not be able to tick or chime, much less speak. Secondly, he must not tell anyone that the clock could talk, especially his new wife. If he did, then the clock might be stolen or misused. Thirdly, he must do whatever the clock told him to do. If he followed the clock's advice, then he would be assured of great personal happiness and riches, too.

Throughout the years, the woman's father had faithfully followed the fairy's instructions. All that had been promised—the happiness and the riches—had come true. The clock would remind the father of many things, like an anniversary, a birthday, and when it was the best time to plant his crops. The father was never late to anything, and all of his decisions were made with the very best of timing.

Sadly, a day came when the father forgot to wind the clock. He woke up late and, realizing he was about to miss a very important date, he rushed out of his great house, trying to make up for lost time. Since the clock was unwound, it could not talk. It could not warn him that it was not a good time to be outside.

A fierce storm was brewing. As the father ran down the path on the way to the village, hurrying to make an important business meeting, a bolt of lightning suddenly struck him in the heart. He fell to the ground and, in a moment, he was dead.

"I'm so sorry I could not warn your father," said the clock. "As it was, all I could do was sit on the mantel and watch the tragedy unfold."

"Not to worry, dear clock. It was not your fault. You had not been wound. Tell me, did my stepmother ever discover that you could talk?" asked the woman.

"No, she never did. After awhile, she put me in a dark closet and forgot all about me. Later, she decided she didn't want me anymore, and so she put me on her garbage heap."

"She did the same thing to me," said the woman.

"Let me give you some advice," said the clock. "It is time for you to make a new life. Yes, you will remember the past, but do not dwell upon its sadness. Instead, make time for those who wish you well. They will reward you over and over for your kindness. In this way you will find happiness."

So the young woman's life changed. She kept the clock in good working order, remembering to wind it every couple of days. She kept its secret and always followed the clock's advice. Throughout her life, she came to learn how important it was to do the right thing at the right time. The woman picked the right man and married him at the right time. She raised her children, giving them both praise and criticism at exactly the right time. She made the right business decisions at just the right time. Most importantly, she took the time to express her appreciation and love to all.

Dear Reader, you may be wondering, what happened to the woman's stepmother and two stepsiblings? Well, sadly, they did all the wrong things at all the wrong times. They never took the time to be kind to each other. And when they finally ran out of time at the end of their lives, they found themselves all alone without even the sound of a ticking clock.

The End

"'How happy we are, alive and free!'"

The Friends

Once there was a cat who was on the last of her nine lives. Her fur had turned gray, and her once lively scampering had become a slow stroll. "Ah, me," she sighed. "Is there nothing left of the former me? Meow, meow," the cat cried out sadly.

Just at that moment, a little mouse poked out her head from her hole. "Why are you crying so? You still have one very good life left!" squeaked the mouse.

"But I have so little left to live with," whined the cat.

"You have more than I have! You are so much greater in size than I, and I bet your teeth are nicer and in greater numbers than mine," said the mouse, flashing the cat a broad smile with a few missing teeth.

"Well, now that you mention it, I guess you are right," purred the cat.

After this beginning exchange of words, the two began what would become the first of many conversations. As you know, dear Reader, cats and mice are not usually on such cordial terms, but these two creatures decided to skip that old predisposition. They decided to meet each day at lunchtime. To avoid the issue of one eating the other, they both decided to bring a bag lunch.

During one of their conversations, these now good friends discovered that they both liked to go on trips to explore the big, beautiful world.

"Why don't we go on a trip together?" suggested the mouse to the cat on one fine day. "I can ride on your back and tell you which way to go."

"Oh, that would be wonderful," said the cat, feeling relief that the mouse would be the navigator of such a venture. You see, the cat had no sense of direction, and as the cat had gotten older, this condition had only gotten worse. On more than one occasion, the cat had even gotten lost coming home to her little burrow in the hills, so the cat was delighted with the arrangements.

"Although you are not fond of water, why don't we go to the ocean shore? I think sitting on the beach and enjoying the ocean waves would be most relaxing. There is nothing so pleasant and reassuring as watching ocean waves coming in, one after another," squeaked the mouse.

"How right you are," purred the cat.

So early one bright and sunny morning, the two started off on their trip together. As agreed, the mouse rode on the back of the cat. Understanding the cat's embarrassment in not knowing which way to go, the mouse, with the utmost tact, whispered gently into the ear of the cat. She told the cat to go twenty steps to the right and then forty steps to the left, and so it went.

When they got to the sea, the cat exclaimed, "Look how big, beautiful, and blue it is!" Feeling poetically inclined, the cat said, "I think I'll write a poem!" And so she did. It went like this:

"Two dear friends
along the sea.
How happy we are,
alive and free!"

Just as the cat finished her verse, a bird swooped down over the heads of the cat and mouse. It chirped, "Say, what are a cat and mouse doing together? Isn't one of you afraid of the other?"

"Why no," squeaked the mouse as loudly as she could.

"We believe in the integration of all species!" shouted the cat. Becoming interested in hearing more, the bird flew down farther and landed on the back of the cat.

"Does this apply to birds?" asked this inquisitive new friend.

"Why yes," said the mouse and the cat together, in perfect harmony.

"Well, that does it," tweeted the bird. "I am definitely joining your little group. I have so much to say, and you seem like the perfect listeners!"

"We will be happy to provide you with all the attention that you require," said the cat and mouse, again in perfect harmony. And so they listened to the first of many tales that the bird had to tell. Waiting politely for a pause in the storytelling, the mouse then led the cat and their new friend, the bird, in a rousing rendition of the cat's poem, which had now become a song:

"Three dear friends
along the sea.
How happy we are,
alive and free!"

After a bit more singing, the three now good friends, went to sleep all huddled together in a cozy cove along the sea.

The next morning, the three were off on their way together to explore their surroundings. The mouse continued to ride on the back of the cat and the bird circled overhead, continuing to chatter about everything under the sun. In the course of all of this verbal outpouring, the cat and mouse learned that the bird was as old as they, and this accounted for the hoarseness the bird sometimes exhibited. But no matter—the cat and mouse continued to listen to the bird.

"Go twenty steps this way, dear cat," whispered the mouse into the ear of the cat as they continued on their way. The mouse continued guiding the cat with the utmost of mathematical precision and consideration. All three of these friends continued on their journey, all feeling very content with the company of each other.

Wanting a change of scenery, the three decided to travel to the Great Forest, which was nearby. This forest had ancient trees that had seen the passage of much time. "Now go this way," whispered the mouse. The small group now made their way down a sandy path, heading inland.

At last the three came to the Great Forest. The cat and mouse looked up, trying to see the tops of the trees, as the bird flew up to see for herself. All the time she chirped down to her friends, telling them all that she saw.

"Our dear friend is most helpful with all the information she gives us," commented the cat to the mouse.

When the bird finally flew down, the three decided to have their lunch. As always, they were careful to eat foods that would not offend any of the sensibilities of those in their party. Today's meal was cheese and bread. This menu particularly delighted the mouse and the bird. As they were eating and exchanging many pleasantries, they heard a crack, like the breaking of a twig.

"Look there!" cried the mouse. All three friends looked into an opening in the trees. There stood a deer.

"I am alone. May I join you?" asked the deer.

The three animals—the cat, the mouse, and the bird—all replied together, "Why yes!"

Then they sang with the deer in four-part harmony:

"Four dear friends
among the trees.
How happy we are,
alive and free!"

The deer smiled and then joined in the munching of the afternoon meal. And so, the four animals spent the rest of the day finding great pleasure in each other's company as they relaxed on the forest floor, talking about a great many things.

As evening began to descend on the forest, the deer said, "Follow me, dear friends. I will show you a place to spend the evening." So this merry, but tired, group followed the deer to a comfortable place to rest. In addition, the deer showed what a good hostess she was in her home of many trees. When they had all nested together in a grassy meadow surrounded by some great oaks, she served them delicious, sparkling water from a nearby stream and some lovely dandelion greens. That night they all slept quite comfortably in their wooded surroundings.

Early the next morning, the group of now four fast friends learned that another animal was about to make their acquaintance. The bird chirped brightly to all that her very good friend, a squirrel, would be joining their party.

"Here she comes!" chirped the bird.

"Hello to all!" sang out the squirrel as she scampered into their camp. All of the animals were amazed at the beautiful necklace of flowers and leaves that hung around the squirrel's neck. She was quite obviously a talented jewelry designer of nature's best.

"Oh, how I wish I could have such a lovely decoration around my neck," lamented the cat. All of the other animals felt the very same way. They also cried out for a trinket of their own. Hearing them, the squirrel quickly made each animal a special lei of flowers and leaves that she put around each of their necks. Then there was a tremendous outpouring of joy for this kind act. The thoughtful squirrel was immediately inducted into the group. They all celebrated by singing:

"Five dear friends
among the trees.
How happy we are,
alive and free!"

After a good amount of talking and laughing, and after their hostess, the deer, served them more refreshments, the whole group of now five friends decided to further explore the forest. The deer and squirrel led the way, with the cat following behind. The mouse, as usual, rode on the back of the cat, and the bird circled overhead.

As they walked, this merry group of five friends meowed, squeaked, chirped, and made all sorts of happy, friendly sounds. To ensure that water was always at hand, the group followed the twists and turns of the forest stream. As a result, no one found themselves thirsty, not even for a moment. The group continued on their way.

"Look!" shouted the squirrel. "What is that there in the stream?"

"Why, it is a beautiful trout jumping up to catch a fly," observed the deer.

"Look again!" cried the bird as she flew over to check on this lovely creature. The trout jumped again, showing to all her great skill and grace in capturing yet another fly.

"I wish I could move that well," sighed the cat.

"Well, you still have a few good moves," whispered the mouse into the cat's ear.

The entire party now decided that they would stop and watch more of this magnificent fish as it continued to leap out of the water for flies. Every time the fish leaped into the air, the whole party cheered for the fish.

Dear Reader, it should be no surprise to you that this merry group of five animals now decided to invite the fish to join their party, which she did, although she was often very busy leaping out of the water and displaying other amazing feats.

"You are like a dancer in the water," said the squirrel, full of admiration.

That night the now six good friends spent a very pleasant evening together, doing their usual thing—what else but talking and laughing a lot! Relaxing in a cozy spot in the woods, they all sang:

"Six dear friends
along the stream.
How happy we are,
alive and free!"

They continued to talk as a full moon rose into the sky. Then their talk turned to a subject more profound.

"Where are we heading?" asked the cat.

"Well, that is a very good question," replied the mouse. And then she added, "Do we have to have a destination? What do the rest of you think about this?"

The bird immediately jumped into the discussion and chirped, "Why, you must always have a destination! Otherwise, what is the point of the journey?"

"Well, I have been traveling with you in what is already my home, the Great Forest. I am already where I need to be," observed the deer.

"Yes, this is my home, too!" added the squirrel.

"Mine, too!" babbled the trout as she rested near the stream's bank.

"Not to worry," commented someone yet unknown to the group.

"Who was that?" squeaked the mouse, looking all about. Now everyone in their party started glancing here and there and asking the same questions: "Who are you?" and "Where are you?"

"Look up!" chirped the bird as she fluttered above the heads of her friends. "Look up!" she repeated. All looked up and there, sitting on a limb of a great tree, sat an owl. She was a bit older than the rest of the party below, but she definitely looked like a kindred spirit.

The owl blinked her eyes and then spoke again, "Not to worry. I think you have already reached your destination."

"But, what do you mean?" queried the bird as she flew up closer to the owl.

"Well, what did you have when you started your journey?" asked the owl.

"No one," replied the cat. One by one, each of the animals answered with the same response: "No one."

"Look around," instructed the owl. "What do you have now?"

All the animals started talking at once. "I have you, dear mouse!" purred the cat.

"Let me return the compliment," squeaked the mouse. "I have you, dear cat!"

"And, I have you both!" sang out the bird. Then the deer, the squirrel, and the fish also joined in with some equally warm words of appreciation for the friendships they now had. The great trees of the forest all smiled and nodded in agreement. They had never heard such a joyful sound as what they were now hearing.

"Since you have given us such a good perspective on where we are, would you like to join our band of friends, dear owl?" asked the cat.

"Why, I would be honored to join you," replied the owl. And so this is how the seven friends came to be. They decided then and there that their group was now complete. All the rest of their days were filled with joy as they talked, laughed, ate, and sang their song:

"Seven dear friends
along the stream.
How happy we are,
alive and free!"

The End

"'You look like a fairy, but where are your wings?'"

A Mother's Love

Once there was a woman who longed to have children of her own. Each night she prayed that she might be blessed as others to experience this special kind of love. Years passed, but with no child. When her husband died, the woman realized that her one great wish would never come true.

"Oh, how I wish I could have even one year of motherhood," cried out this very sad woman.

Now it so happened that an equally sad fairy lived nearby in the neighborhood. This fairy's grief stemmed from the fact that she had been born without wings. While all her fellow fairies flitted from flower to flower on their beautiful wings, this fairy had to walk through brier and brush to get to where she wanted to go.

"If only I could have a pair of wings like the other fairies!" she lamented.

Well, as fortune would have it, the path of the sad woman and that of the sad fairy crossed one day. The fairy was trudging past the woman's house when she heard crying coming from within.

"Who cries so?" wondered the fairy. So, she walked up to the door and knocked on it. In a moment, the door opened.

"Who is there?" asked the woman who had been crying. She looked all about, but saw no one.

"Look down," said the fairy, who was only three inches tall.

"Why, there you are!" exclaimed the woman. "You look like a fairy, but where are your wings?"

The fairy was irritated by the woman's comment, but she kept her anger in check. A plan was beginning to hatch in her head.

"May I come in?" asked the fairy.

"Of course you can!" said the woman, quickly drying her eyes. She was a very sorrowful woman, but she had not lost her desire to welcome anyone who came to her door. She graciously offered the fairy some tea and honey cakes.

"Why, thank you," said the fairy as the refreshments disappeared into her tiny mouth. "Tell me," said the fairy. "Why do you weep? I heard your sobs as I walked past your door."

"I cry for the children I never had," said the woman in a very quiet voice. "My husband is dead and I am now old. My hope for children fades with each passing day."

"Sorry to hear this," said the fairy, "but perhaps I can help you."

"Oh, could you?" asked the woman, brightening. "But how? What I want is not possible." The mind of the fairy was now working at hyper-speed.

"Maybe not for a mortal, but it is certainly well within the power of a fairy, even one without wings," said the fairy. "Tell me, why do you want children?"

"I want to experience the love a mother has for her very own," said the woman.

"Done!" said the fairy as she waved her wand over the woman. "By tomorrow your wish will be granted. But . . . there is one thing I need from you. After fifteen years from today, you must agree to lose everything you have. Is that okay?"

Without hesitation, the woman said "Yes!" to the fairy. She was now filled with hope for a new life. The fairy smiled, thinking about her new life, too. She thought about the *Great Book of Fairy Spells*. In this volume was listed Spell Number 4568921. It stated that any wish not within the power of a fairy would be granted if a fairy could get a human to agree to lose everything. Only in this way could the fairy get her wings, since wing wishing was not a faculty possessed by fairies.

The little creature left the woman's home, delighted with the agreement she had gotten. She found herself wondering what color her wings would be.

The woman was also happy. She found herself singing as she made preparations for her children. After a flurry of cleaning and cooking, she finally went to bed. The woman tried to sleep, but there was none to be had. She was just too excited as she lay in her bed waiting for the next day.

Early in the morning, she heard the sound of children's voices coming from her kitchen. The woman's heart began to beat with great joy.

"Is my wish finally fulfilled? Are these the sounds of my very own children?" With great excitement, she sprang out of her bed and hurried in the direction of the voices.

There, standing in her kitchen, were a golden-haired boy and a girl with long, flowing brown hair. "Good morning, dear mother," said the children. Their voices were like the sounds of angels.

The woman, now a mother, quickly gathered up the children in her arms, hugging them and saying, "Good morning, my sweet children! Let me get your breakfast!"

The woman's life now became a happy one. She loved her children beyond the love of an ordinary mother. Everything that she could do for them, she did. She cooked them delicious meals, sewed them beautiful clothes, and filled their heads with stories and, of course, their ABCs and numbers.

"I have the most wonderful children in the world! They are all that I have ever hoped for," she told herself every day.

The years went flying by. Soon the fifteenth year since the children first appeared would be here. The woman remembered what she had promised the fairy. But, not to worry! She had thought of a way to fulfill her obligation. She would give the fairy a great pile of gifts that she had made. There were beautiful garments, each carefully sewed with no openings for wings, as she remembered that the fairy was lacking these usual fairy parts. She also baked a great quantity of her best cakes and other very delicious treats for the fairy.

On the eve of the fifteenth year, the fairy appeared before the woman. "As promised, it is now time for you to lose everything," said the fairy.

"But look at all that I have for you, kind fairy," said the woman as she pointed to the great mound of gifts.

"Why, thank you," said the fairy as she gathered up all that had been made for her. Sadly, dear Reader, the fairy had more in mind. She knew that if she were to procure her wings, the woman would have to give up everything she had. "Goodbye," said the fairy as she left with a great pack on her back.

"Goodbye, dear fairy!" said the woman, breathing a sigh of relief. The woman now believed that her promise had been fulfilled. She called for her children, now young adults, to come to dinner. The three sat down and, as usual, began eating their dinner and sharing the news of the day.

"I have chopped wood for you, dear mother," said the young man.

"I have sewed you a cloak to keep you warm, sweet mother," said the young woman.

After washing the dishes, locking the door, and, of course, giving each other good-night kisses, this little family retired to their respective beds.

During the night, the mother's dreams were filled with a strange foreboding. But the next day she brushed aside her unease and rose from her bed to make the morning meal. First, she reached for some wood to start a fire in her stove, but where there had been a neat pile of wood the night before, there stood only an empty rack.

"No matter," she thought. "I can quickly chop some more wood."

She went outside to complete the task. As she lifted an ax, the words of the fairy reverberated in her mind: "You must agree to lose everything you have." At that very moment, the woman dropped the ax and fell hard onto the ground.

She cried out in pain, "Help! Help!" The mother expected her children to come running to help her, but instead they continued to sleep in their beds. Realizing that they were not coming, she struggled to her feet and hobbled into the house. "Help, help, children!" she cried. Her children finally did rise from their beds, but when they learned that their mother wanted them to chop wood, they drew back in horror.

"You want us to work?!" they cried.

"Not me!" shouted the son.

"Not me!" shouted the daughter.

Then both children whined, "When are you fixing our breakfast?" The mother could not believe her ears. Her children's lack of caring frightened her. Still, the mother struggled to make their breakfast, even without any wood for a fire.

"I don't like cold cereal!" complained the daughter.

"I want hot tea!" demanded the son.

The day went on, with the children bickering about this and that. Also, more things began disappearing. The woman found that her cow was gone, and then she discovered that her chickens had wandered off. So there wasn't any milk, nor were there any eggs!

Plates and cups began to crack and then to break into pieces. The table and chairs wobbled and then fell to the floor. The complaints of the children continued. The woman's hair began to gray, and her face was now a collection of wrinkles. The children now found their mother to be a most disagreeable sight. Feeling their revulsion, the woman remembered the words of the fairy: "You must agree to lose everything you have."

The woman cried out to the fairy: "Please, dear fairy, I am losing all! Please come and help me!" The woman was now sobbing. "Please help me, dear fairy!"

Hearing her words, the fairy did finally appear.

"What do you want?" asked the fairy.

"This day I have lost many things. I fear I am losing my children. They are not at all as they were. I hardly know them. They only look at me with disgust."

"Well, I'm sorry to hear this, but a deal is a deal! If I am to get my wings, you must lose everything."

Just then, the woman's children entered the house.

"Mother, we have something to tell you. Since you are such a fright, one that we can't bear to look upon, we are leaving you. Our new friend, who is very wealthy, has offered us a wonderful new home, full of the comforts you can no longer provide. We just came by to get our things." The two children quickly collected all that their mother had given them and then left her without a kiss or even a farewell.

The mother cried out in great pain, "My children! My children!"

The house began to shake. Both the mother and the fairy had to hurry outside. It was a great earthquake! Everything that the woman still had was now shaking and, with one final jolt, all came crashing down. As the house fell, part of it landed on the woman.

The mother now lay dying. She saw that the fairy was unharmed. Just then she heard a great tinkling of bells and then a mighty "Puff!" Two beautiful blue wings now appeared on the shoulders of the fairy.

"I have my wings! At last, I have my wings!" exclaimed the fairy.

"But what about me? Can you not help me?" cried out the woman.

"Well, I already did," said the fairy. "I'm sorry you now have nothing, but you did get what you wished for!" With these last words, the fairy disappeared.

The woman tried to escape, but it was no use. Sadly, dear Reader, she sobbed and then quietly closed her eyes as her life slipped away.

The End

"…the long road of the man and the short one of the woman crossed at one point."

The Heart

The man was traveling down a long road. He was uncertain where it led, but he felt sure he would find what he was looking for at the end of it.

A woman was traveling down a road, too, but her road was a short one. Unlike the man, she knew where it would take her. She was on her way to her small cottage. She had just spent the day in the nearby village, selling her handmade cloaks and capes.

Now it so happened that the long road of the man and the short one of the woman crossed at one point. And, by chance, the man and the woman happened to approach this crossing at the same time. When the man saw the woman, he thought he would ask if she knew of a place he might stay for the evening. He was very tired and could go no farther down his long road.

He asked, "Young woman, do you know of a place I might lodge this evening? I have traveled far and am in great need of some rest."

The woman looked at the man and said, "Sir, there is no place near, but if you like, I can put you up in my cottage for a night. I often take pity on poor, tired travelers, and you certainly look like one." The man was taken aback by the woman's boldness, but he felt relieved to be offered a place to rest. As he looked at the woman, he was intrigued by her soft brown eyes and long blond hair.

"Well," said the woman, "are you coming or not?" With this, she turned and started walking quickly toward her cottage.

The man called out, "Wait! I'm coming!" He had to run to catch up to her. When he was by her side, he said, "How kind you are. I can't tell you how glad I am to be offered a place of shelter. I have come a very long way today."

"Where are you going?" asked the woman.

"I'm not sure," answered the man, "but, I'm certain I will know it when I come to it."

The woman thought the man's words were strange, but she said nothing. She knew not everyone knows where they are heading.

Soon the two came to the woman's home. She opened the door and pointed to a cot for the man. Then she asked, "Are you hungry? You may have some of my evening meal, if you like. It is simple, but it will fill you."

"Why, thank you," replied the man. "I'm sure your dinner will be a feast!"

The man watched the woman prepare the meal as he rested on the cot. He found himself enjoying her every movement, from the cutting of the vegetables to the setting of the table. Then he remembered the bottle of wine in his pack.

"May I offer you some wine to go with the meal?" he asked.

The woman turned to him and smiled. "Why, that would be lovely. I seldom have wine in the cottage because it is so dear, but I certainly do enjoy it."

The man reached over and pulled up his pack. In an instant, he produced a bottle of wine. As he surveyed the dinner on the table, he said, "This is the best meal I have seen in a long while!" Then, with a flourish, he presented the wine to the woman.

The two had a wonderful time eating the woman's vegetables and bread and savoring the man's wine. The meal was truly a feast.

Time passed, and the man and the woman shared the telling of many stories. Then the woman said, "Good night," and disappeared into a back bedroom. The man was left to himself. He thought it was too early to retire, but eventually he laid himself down on the cot and fell asleep.

The next morning, the woman was up early preparing breakfast. The man could smell bacon and eggs cooking. He found himself looking forward to the next meal. He had forgotten how much he liked to eat. During his journey down his long road, he seldom had an opportunity to eat home cooking. Tavern food was all that had been available. It really could not compare with the wonderful aroma coming from the kitchen.

"Good morning," he said to the woman.

Then she turned toward the man, asking, "Do you always sleep so late? It is nearly mid-morning."

"Oh," observed the man. "I guess you are right. I always sleep late in the morning. My custom is to stay up late in the evening, unlike yours."

"Oh," said the woman, blushing. She turned and hastened to complete the breakfast.

This time the man remembered the tea leaves that he had in his pack. "Would you care for some tea to go with the meal?" he asked.

"Why, that would be delightful," she replied.

"I think you will really like this," he said. "It comes from a faraway place that is known for its teas." The woman smiled, took the tea leaves, and in no time at all had a pot of tea ready to go with their breakfast.

Again, the two had an enjoyable time at their meal. So, it is not surprising that the man decided he must extend his visit. He asked if he could stay longer, and the woman said, "You may, but you will have to work for your keep. Beware! You may be called upon to wash the dishes and sweep the floor!"

The man smiled. "It will be my pleasure."

Several days and then weeks passed with the man and woman spending many happy hours talking and sharing the tasks that had to be done around the cottage. The man became so involved with the woman's life that he even began to help her sew the cloaks and capes that she sold in the village. Life became so pleasant for both of them, dear Reader, that the man and woman fell in love.

However, one day the man found himself remembering the long road that he had been traveling down when he first met the woman. He remembered that he had been looking for something at the end of it. What, he still did not know. As the days went by, that something for which he had been seeking began to nag at him. It would not leave him alone. Something at the end of the long road was demanding his attention. He could bear it no longer. He turned to the woman and said, "I must leave. Something I cannot name is calling me. I must find it or go mad."

The woman was shaken by the man's words, but she calmly said, "If this is what you must do, then you must go. I do not want you to go mad." The man was relieved to hear the woman's words, for he loved her and really didn't want to hurt her with his leaving.

"You must do one thing for me," she murmured. "I will be back to explain." She went into her room and then, after a long while, returned to the man. In her hands she held a box about the size of an apple. It was covered with fabric and was held together by neat little stitches.

"Please take this," she said. "When you are at the end of your long road, undo the stitches and look inside the box."

The man studied the woman's face and saw that her eyes were very sad and that her cheeks were very pale. He could not understand why the woman would give him this box, but he agreed to take it and do as she asked. He promised to open it when he came to the end of his road.

With a final kiss, the man and woman parted. The man once again traveled down his long road, and the woman once again traveled down her short one.

Many months passed as the man traveled down his road. There seemed to be no end to it. The farther he traveled, the longer it seemed to become. He wondered if he would ever find that yet unknown thing that was calling to him. Suddenly one day, the man did come to the end of his road. He looked everywhere to find that which he was seeking. Nowhere could he see anything that might be it. There was only an old man sitting on a stump. He was smoking a pipe; a cloudy ring circled over his head.

Not knowing what else to do, the man walked over to the fellow and asked, "Old man, I have traveled to the end of this long road looking for some unknown thing. And now that I have come to the end of it, I see nothing."

"Young man," said the old gentleman, "you are just within sight of that which you seek." With these words, the old man pointed to the man's pack. Then he spoke again. "Open the box that the woman gave you, and you will find what you are looking for."

The man took the box out of his pack and carefully undid the stitches that held it together. The fabric fell lightly to the ground. Carefully, the man lifted the top of the box. Inside he saw what the woman had given him. He now realized why her eyes had been so sad and her cheeks so pale at their parting. She had given him her heart.

The man was overwhelmed by her gift. How could she have given him something so precious? It must mean that the woman had a very deep love for him. The man sat down, badly shaken. Then he turned to the old man and asked, "Why did I have to travel all the way to the end of this very long road?"

"Well," replied the old man, "sometimes you have to travel a long way before you realize that what you are seeking is very near." With these words, the old man disappeared. The younger man turned from the end of his long road and so began his trek back to the woman. All he could think about was seeing her again.

When he finally came to her cottage, he knocked eagerly on the door. "Come in," said a faint little voice. The man quickly went inside and found the woman cooking the evening meal. Although she was very frail and pale, the woman looked beautiful.

The man moved closer to her. He reached into his pack and pulled out the box that she had given him. Opening it, he gave her back her heart. The color returned to the woman's cheeks and her eyes became happy ones.

Then the man spoke. "From now on, your road will be my road. I have found what I have been seeking. It is you!"

With these words, the man kissed the woman with a kiss of true love. And so, dear Reader, from that day on, the woman and the man traveled down the same road together.

The End

"She sent her mother a letter with the simple message, 'Mother, I love you.'"

The Last Letter

The mother and daughter were very close. When the father died suddenly, it was the daughter who consoled her grief-stricken mother. The girl cherished her mother with a deep and abiding love.

There were other members of the family, and they also played a part in the mother's life. Sadly, their intentions were not pure, like those of their little sister. They played the role of doting children, but a closer examination revealed a darker side to these children, one involving black magic. Their intentions were driven by a desire for gold and precious jewels. These the mother had in large amounts, neatly piled in her great vault.

"We must find a way to remove our sister from the affections of our mother by using some of our special arts. In this way we will not have to share any of our inheritance with her. Perhaps, by carefully planting lies, this can be done," said the brother, full of evil intent.

"I think this could be managed," said the equally evil older sister. "After all, our younger sister is such a naïve one. She knows nothing of magic. She will not realize what we have done until it is too late!"

So the two began to carry out their cruel plan. First they made up a brew of magical, very believable lies. This they made deep down in the brother's crowded cellar. Being a pack rat, he had all the required ingredients, such as toad's ear, rotten camel's breath, and poisoned mushrooms from a whispering pine tree. Every day they secretly put some of this brew into their mother's tea and so clouded her mind with many falsehoods. In this way, frightening and quite untrue thoughts about the younger daughter began to poison the mother. Thoughts like, "She does not love you, dear mother. She only cares about your pile of gold and your precious jewels!" and "She will hurt you!" filled the mother's mind.

At first the mother did not believe these vicious lies. But because they pursued her with ever increasing power, relentlessly filling her ears about the dire consequences of keeping her younger daughter, the mother finally began to weaken. Eventually, she became afraid. These scheming children even convinced their mother through their venomous brew that the younger daughter would someday bring about her death. So because of this black magic, there came a day when the mother gave permission to her son and older daughter to take their younger sister far away.

Early one morning, they dragged the younger sister from the house. After many days of forcing her to walk over hill and dale, they finally brought her into a very dark forest. Then the wicked brother and sister gave their younger sister some of their evil brew to drink. The mind of the younger sister became filled with thoughts that she had no home, that she had nothing, not even a coat, and that she was even without a namesake.

Just before they left, the older brother and sister made sure that their younger sister was also tormented with warnings that she should never return to their mother's home and never communicate with their mother in any way.

"If you do, you will surely kill her!" they told their sister. The cruelty of this lie cut deeply into their sister's soul. Never did she want to hurt her mother. Was she really such a horrible person? Frightened by their words, she promised never to see her mother again. She still didn't know why or how she could be such a threat to her mother. She only knew that she didn't want to harm her in any way. Having completed their work, this evil pair now left, leaving their younger sister all alone.

As the young woman lay on the floor of the woods, she cried many tears. She agonized over being abandoned. Why had her family treated her so badly? She must be a truly awful creature!

Then she heard a voice coming from within the forest. It was a good-hearted wood nymph who lived in a great oak tree. It said, "You are not the person they describe. You are a good and dear human who rightly deserves the love of others. Drink from the nearby stream, and your head will be cleared of all the evil lies that are hurting you."

The younger sister stood up and did just as the wood nymph directed. She went to the nearby stream. Kneeling down, she drank from it. A great feeling of relief spilled over her mind. She was now freed from the lies that had tormented her!

Then she heard the wood nymph speak again. "Once your head is clear, you must find your happiness far away from those who would harm you. Go beyond this forest; find your peace and happiness in a little valley."

So the younger daughter did as the wood nymph instructed. She traveled past the forest and found a home in a little valley. The people there grew to appreciate and love the kind and sweet ways of the unwanted daughter. Eventually, she found friends who filled the hole left by her missing family. She even found the love of a very good man. Her life now seemed complete. Her wealth was not measured in gold or jewels, but in the sweet embraces of the people who loved her.

Still, even with the passage of many happy years, the woman was haunted by the loss of her mother. Again and again, she would wake up feeling this loss. Early one morning, the woman rose crying as she related to her husband yet another dream about her mother. Never in all this time had her mother come looking for her or even sent her a letter. It was as if her mother considered her younger daughter dead.

The pain of this loss would not go away. Again and again, the daughter woke with the same sadness. Finally her husband, being a wise and caring fellow, suggested to her, "Why don't you send your mother a letter, one with the simplest of messages. Just write, 'I love you.' I think it would make you, and possibly your mother, feel better."

The woman did as her husband suggested. She sent her mother a letter with the simple message, "Mother, I love you." At the bottom of the card she signed, "Your younger daughter." Twice a year she would send a letter with the same message. This went on for many years. Sadly, the daughter never received a response.

What did the mother think of the letters? Well, let me tell you, dear Reader. The first time the mother received a letter from her younger daughter, she almost threw it away. Surely, this daughter would have nothing kind to say to her. How could she? The mother had done the worst thing any mother can do to her child—deny it love.

Pausing a moment, the mother's curiosity and secret longing for her missing child now motivated her. It had been some time since she had drunk of the evil brew. Her mind had cleared, and she had been feeling pangs of love for her younger daughter. However, she was now very much afraid of her two older children. She had learned of their dabblings in black magic. Still, she decided to open the letter from her younger daughter. Inside she saw what she had so much longed for—a message of love. The mother cried. She couldn't tell if her tears were from happiness or sadness.

A lot of time passed. Twice a year the mother would get the same message from her younger daughter. Each letter always read, "Mother, I love you." Fearing her two other children, the mother kept the existence of these letters a secret.

On her deathbed, as the mother was gasping for her breath, her two children were busy making arrangements for their mother's burial.

"What precious things our mother has acquired during her lifetime!" commented the older daughter. "I can hardly wait to adorn myself with Mother's beautiful jewels!" she exclaimed.

"Yes," said the brother with excitement. "I will be able to leave my heavily mortgaged home for Mother's fine mansion. What a wonderful day that will be!"

The mother finally breathed her last breath. Noting her demise, the two children moved quickly to make the final arrangements. All was done neatly and efficiently.

Later, as they cleared away their mother's things, they spied a simple metal box near her bed. It was not made of any precious metal like gold or silver. No precious stones were encrusted on the top. Eagerly, the two children opened the box. To their great disappointment, there was no treasure inside, only a collection of old letters tied together with a red ribbon. On top was a note with the following instructions: "To be opened by my two children at the time of my death. Please return these letters to my younger daughter." The note was signed and dated by their mother, apparently, on her last day of life.

"Oh, confound it!" said the brother. "I was so hoping for something valuable inside this old box. All we have here are some old letters from our stupid younger sister!" he complained.

"Well," said his sister, "perhaps, we can have some fun with these letters. Let's go visit our younger sister and flaunt our newly acquired wealth in front of her. After our younger sister gets a good look at us, especially at Mother's jewels, we can tell her that Mother did leave her something."

"Yes," said her brother, catching on to his sister's plan. "And as soon as her face brightens, we can throw all these old letters at her! Ha, ha! This will be the best trick yet that we have pulled on our little sister!"

His sister nodded with enthusiasm. "Just give me a moment to deck myself out with some of Mother's lovely gems!"

"Okay, Sister. But let's not delay on our mission of mischief! I can hardly wait to begin!"

In very short order, the evil duo was on their way to their younger sister's house. They traveled over hill and dale and through the forest; at last, they came to the little valley where their younger sister lived.

"Oh, why did she have to live so far away?" complained the older sister.

"How inconvenient for those who have mischief on their minds!" added the brother.

Arriving at the home of their younger sister, this no-good pair marched up to her front door and banged on it in a most disagreeable way.

"Open up!" they demanded. The door opened, and there stood their younger sister.

"Mother has asked us to bring you something," hissed the older sister as she adjusted the large ruby necklace around her throat.

"Yes, we have something very special for you, dear sister," added the brother with a smirk.

Just as they had predicted, the younger sister brightened up with a smile. "At last," the younger sister thought, "my mother has remembered me!"

Sadly, her happiness was dashed by her brother throwing the letters at her and saying in the coldest of voices, "Our dear mother gives you back your old letters that she never wanted! In her dying words she told us that she never loved you. She only loved me and my older sister. All we have ever felt for you, dear sister, is disgust!"

It was as if the younger sister had been struck with an arrow that went straight through her heart. She fell backward, collapsing onto the ground. Hearing the commotion, her husband rushed to her aid.

Seeing his wife's ashen face and the haughty faces of her brother and sister, he shouted, "Be gone, you vile creatures! Leave, or you will have to deal with me! I know all about your black magic. It will not work on me!" Not accustomed to being challenged, the brother and sister fled. For, dear Reader, as many of us know, these sorts of folk are cowards. They will always fly in the face of the true and brave-hearted. Off they ran as fast as their legs could carry them.

The husband held his wife in his arms. She was now crying uncontrollably. Quickly, he carried her inside their home and laid her down on the bed. She continued to sob.

"Please, my dear, do not think about the cruel words of your brother and sister. Remember that I love you and so do many others. Your brother and sister are so full of evil that they can only find mean and untrue things to say about others. Please calm yourself."

Wanting to prevent any further attacks on his family, the husband ran back to the front door to bolt it. Seeing the letters strewed outside on the ground, he quickly scooped them up and then secured the door. Returning to his wife, he tried to console her, but her tears poured out without ending.

"What can I do to help?" he asked in desperation. This caring and sweet man felt helpless as he continued to hold his wife in his arms, telling her over and over again that he loved her and for her to please be comforted. Yet, she continued to cry.

Not knowing what else to do, he decided to read the letters that had been thrown so cruelly at his wife. Perhaps they would give him a clue on how to end his wife's torment.

He began to read the letters. As he had advised his wife, her message to her mother was, in each of the letters, a simple one. "Mother, I love you. Your younger daughter." He continued to read the letters until he got to the last one. Again, he read the same message his wife had written over and over.

"How tragic," he thought. "In all of the years she had written her mother, not one response had she received from her." He turned over his wife's last letter and was startled at what he saw. It was a message from his wife's mother! He read it quickly and then went straight to his wife, who was still crying.

"My dear! I have discovered a message from your mother! She wrote it on the backside of your last letter to her!"

His wife stopped sobbing and sat up, in shock. "Read it to me!" she stammered.

Her husband read aloud the following:

"My younger daughter,

I am so sorry for the grief I have given you. As I lie on my bed, with death near, I know I must try to find a way to tell you that I do love you. You will always be my daughter. I hope in some way you will see these words.

Your mother"

The daughter began to cry again. Dear Reader, she didn't know if her tears were from happiness or sadness, but she did know that now her suffering would finally come to an end. Her mother had given her the greatest treasure of all on the backside of the last letter—a message of love.

The End

"…this once-again common woman fled to the Great Forest."

True Love

Once there was a kingdom that had the custom of honoring a commoner at the Royal Ball held once a year at the King's palace. A member of the Royal Family would select a commoner to be among the members of the Royal Court on this special occasion. This year's selection was a young woman who lived in a small cottage near the Great Forest. She had been chosen by the Prince, who had seen her one day as she was picking flowers in a nearby meadow.

The Prince had gotten off his beautiful white horse and had walked over to the woman. He had been charmed by her simple beauty and her smile. Thinking of the ball, he had said, using his most courtly voice, "Dear maiden, would you please accept my invitation to the Royal Ball?"

She had instantly replied, "Sir, I would be honored to accept your kind offer." The woman had felt magic in the air.

"Splendid! My Royal Carriage will be by at nine o'clock to pick you up for the ball," he had told her. Then the Prince had waved goodbye and was once again riding his beautiful white horse.

"This turn of events is a dream come true!" had exclaimed the young woman. "But, oh my! What should I wear?" She did not have any fancy ball gowns in her closet. Then she had remembered her one very nice peasant dress. She could put flowers in her hair and wear her mother's string of beads around her neck. Not to worry! After all, the Prince had invited her and magic was in the air. In no time at all, she was ready for the ball.

This brings us, dear Reader, to the main event—the ball! As promised, the Royal Carriage arrived promptly at nine o'clock. A coachman sprang to the ground and helped her into the carriage. Then, with a crack of his whip, the driver drove off in the direction of the palace. Great excitement filled the woman. She would be dancing with members of the Royal Court! She wondered if the Prince would be among her dancing partners.

In no time at all, the carriage arrived at the front gate of the palace. The coachman once again sprang from the coach, and then escorted the woman to the entrance. A large door opened, and the woman was suddenly thrust into a whole new world—the great Court of the King!

All of her senses were heightened by what she saw. Elegantly dressed dancers moved gracefully across the polished floor of the ballroom. But what most caught the attention of the young woman was the beautiful music coming from the Royal Band. She had never heard such glorious sounds. In particular, she admired the brilliance of a trumpet that now heralded her arrival into the ballroom with a spirited fanfare.

A Royal Guard escorted her into the large hall. Stopping at the entrance, he tapped his mighty staff twice. Then he announced with authority, "May I present a lady from near the Great Forest. She is our honored commoner for the evening."

The Prince hurried up to her side and, bowing, he said, "My beautiful commoner, may I have this dance?"

The woman blushed with delight, replying, "You may, dear Prince."

But the young woman did not know any of the steps to the dance or any of the others done by the members of the Court. She began to panic, not knowing what to do.

At that very moment, she heard the sound of the trumpet. It was telling her with its musical notes which way to move. Quickly, she realized that the trumpet would guide her through all of the intricate movements of the dance. She smiled with relief. Thank goodness for the trumpet!

All during the ball, it was the trumpet that was her best friend, helping her to step and turn at exactly the right time. Her evening became a great triumph. Everyone at the ball smiled at her, marveling at her remarkable dancing ability.

"And, she is only a commoner," exclaimed all the people of the Court. The Prince was also very impressed. He smiled at the woman as he danced every dance with her. Carefully, the woman listened to the trumpet as it continued to guide her movements.

Later that same evening, the Prince kissed the woman and then asked her to marry him the very next day. The woman had been swept off her feet, and so she said, without hesitation, "Yes, my Prince!" So, a Royal Wedding was hastily arranged. In short order, the young woman from near the Great Forest was now a Princess.

But being a Princess is not an easy task, especially for someone so young and inexperienced as this woman. There were so many protocols to observe as a member of the Court, and even more if you were a member of the Royal Family. Each time this new Princess made a mistake, the Prince would correct her. All day long all she heard was, "No! No! You have made another mistake! Do it this way!"

The members of the Court began to notice all the mistakes that the new Princess was making. "Well," they said, "what can you expect from a commoner? The Prince should have known this would happen. He should get rid of her before she embarrasses him and the whole Court any further!" And so the talking continued at the Royal Court.

The woman began to wither under all the complaints she was now receiving from everyone. She was like a flower when it is pelted by a downfall of rain. Each insult beat down upon her natural cheerfulness and good spirits. It is not surprising that she became very sad. In desperation, she searched the palace, seeking a place of refuge. At last she found a little corner of the palace where she would be free from criticism—the music chamber. She found solace hiding in one of the many small practice rooms.

As she sat quietly in one of these rooms, she heard the festive tunes of a trumpet playing. The sounds were so bright and cheery that the spirits of the Princess began to lift. She even found herself smiling. From then on, the Princess made a point of visiting the music chamber every day. By listening to the music of the trumpet, she found a way to endure the daily barbs she was receiving from the Prince and the other members of the Court.

But who was the man who played the trumpet? The Princess was now struck by a great curiosity—who was he? She remembered it was this very same trumpet player who had saved her from a misstep at the ball.

The very next day, the Princess hurried to the music chamber in search of the trumpet player, but she could not find him. She could hear him playing, but he played a kind of hide-and-seek with her, darting all around the hall. Just when she thought she had found him, he would be gone. This game went on for many days.

"Where oh where is my trumpet player? Why does he hide from me?" she wondered. "He must be a very shy fellow," she thought.

Sadly, the Princess was now beset with the reality that her Royal Marriage to the Prince was going to be terminated. Everyone in the Court, including the Prince, had decided that the Princess was not fit for the job as Royal Consort. She must be returned to her original status—single and common. With a quick decree from the King, an act of Royal Dissolution was completed.

The no-longer-a-Princess was devastated. How could her Prince treat her so badly? Was love so fleeting? Feeling very ashamed and unwanted, this once-again common woman fled to the Great Forest. She was so distraught that she ran without looking where she was going. Deeper and deeper into the forest she flew. The trees became darker and darker.

After going a long way, the woman stopped and, glancing all around, she saw that she was now lost. She realized that her prospects were not good. She would probably be eaten by the cruel beasts that lurked in the forest. The woman threw herself down upon the forest floor and began to cry, sobbing over the misery of her soon-to-be short life.

Then she heard a familiar sound in the distance. It was the trumpet! It seemed to call out to her, telling her to come to it. She picked herself up and began to walk in the direction of the music.

Following the sweet, encouraging sounds, the woman finally found her trumpet player. A young man, wearing the uniform of the Royal Band, stood before her. He had blond hair and clear blue eyes. He greeted her with a fanfare as he would have greeted the greatest monarch.

"My dear young woman," he said, "I cannot offer you riches, but I can offer you something far better—true love."

And so the trumpet player and the once-upon-a-time-Princess were married. There was no Royal Carriage, no Great Ballroom, and no elegantly dressed dancers; but there was an abundance of family members and friends who celebrated this simple wedding. Dear Reader, I know you will be glad to learn that this couple lived happily ever after.

The End

"'Welcome to the wonders of Fairy Land!'"

The Wonders of Fairy Land

Once there was a woman who had a special gift. She could look into a person's heart and know what would help that person. It could be something very small, like smiling at a stranger, or something very large, like giving a loved one years of caring. Throughout her life, the woman had offered all kinds of helpfulness to all kinds of people.

Now, some people recognized the basic goodness of the woman's deeds, but there were others who did not. They would sometimes toss aside her special gift or accept it without one word of thanks. Still, she continued helping others.

One day the woman met a boy who was crying. He was all alone on a dusty road. His clothes were torn and his hands and feet were dirty. The woman stopped.

"Are you hurt?" she asked.

"No," said the boy, "but I am very hungry."

"Not to worry," said the woman as she unwrapped her lunch and gave it to him. He quickly gobbled it down.

"Feeling better?" she asked.

"Yes, much better. But, I'm still lost," cried the boy.

"Well, let me help you find your way." So, the woman picked up the boy and, in no time at all, she found his home. His parents were happy to have their son back, but in all the excitement of his homecoming, they forgot to thank the woman. "No matter," she said to herself as she waved good-bye to the boy and his parents.

As she continued on her way, she next encountered a young woman sitting under a tree near the road. She held her head in her hands and was rocking back and forth. She seemed to be very troubled over something.

The woman stopped and asked, "What is the matter?"

"My husband is a very bad man! He does not understand my desires at all!" cried out this younger woman.

"Well, do you understand his?" asked the woman.

"Why, that is a stupid thing for you to say!" snapped the younger woman. "I am young and beautiful! Surely, this is enough reason for him to fulfill all of my wishes." With this remark, she tossed her head with an air of defiance.

"You will experience great unhappiness with this point of view," observed the woman. "It takes two to make a happy home."

The younger woman was now very angry with the woman. She stood up and then, turning on her heel, left in a huff. As the younger woman walked, all she could hear in her mind was, "It takes two to make a happy home!" These words repeated themselves over and over again. So, by the time she got home to her husband, these words had actually sunk in. She followed the woman's advice and eventually did have a happy home.

The woman continued on her way. She had traveled some distance when she decided to stop at a nearby tavern. She needed to rest her tired bones. With a few coins, she was able to get a meal and a room. Sinking into a well-used bed, she fell into a deep sleep, dreaming about all the people she had helped.

The next morning, she woke to the sound of screams. Quickly, she dressed and rushed out of her room to see what was going on. A young girl was screaming in the middle of the tavern's dining area.

"Stop your yelling, you stupid girl!" hollered the tavern's innkeeper. The girl continued to scream, and so this innkeeper picked her up and threw her out the door. "Now we can have some peace," he sighed. "Drinks for all!"

Everyone within earshot rushed up to the bar to collect their free drinks. "To the innkeeper!" they all shouted as they lifted their glasses.

The woman looked at this scene and sadly shook her head. "But what about the girl?" she wondered. Without further hesitation, she hurried outside. There she saw the young girl crying and uttering words that were almost unintelligible. She approached the girl, saying, "Hello. Can I help you?"

The girl looked at her with disbelief, saying, "Why would you want to help me? Nobody likes me."

"Well, I see that you need a friend," said the woman. The two began to talk. The woman listened with great patience to the many sorrows of the girl. During her whole life, she had never had a friend. In desperation, she had screamed and had a fit any time a person approached her. This accounted for the scene in the tavern.

After awhile, the girl calmed down, and she was even able to smile. The woman now invited her to join her for lunch at the tavern. At first the innkeeper didn't want to serve the girl, but then the woman persuaded him. So, the girl and her new friend enjoyed several hours together as they talked and ate their afternoon meal. When they were done, the woman took the girl back to her home and promised to return once a month to take her to lunch.

Many years passed, and the woman aged with each passing day. Her face was now covered with many wrinkles, her body was bent over, and her step was now much slower. Still, she continued to help people in small and large ways. Sometimes she was thanked, but often she was not.

One day, as the woman sat on a stump along a road, a beautiful fairy suddenly appeared before her. This was most surprising to the woman, as you, dear Reader, might expect.

"Can I help you, little fairy?" asked the woman.

"Why, that is a sweet offer," replied the fairy. "But, it is I who has something for you."

"Oh my!" said the woman, "Whatever could it be?"

"It is a golden key," said the fairy, and in an instant a key appeared in the fairy's tiny hand. Stepping closer, the fairy said, "Kind and helpful lady, please take this key, and when you see a golden door, you must unlock it." The woman took the key, and in a flash the fairy was gone. The woman looked all around, but she saw no golden door. Not knowing what else to do, she put the key into her apron pocket for safekeeping.

The old-getting-even-older woman continued on down the path of her life, giving help to those who she saw needed a helping hand. Sometimes, all it took was a wink and a smile. Other times, she had to make a great effort to help someone with a more serious problem. As time went by, it became harder and harder to continue this work, but the woman struggled on.

One day she realized that her days of helping others had come to an end. She had given everything she had. She was now all alone, breathing her last breaths.

Just as her world began to fade, a golden door appeared before her. The woman remembered the words of the fairy. Realizing that she must hurry, she stood up and took the golden key from her apron pocket. Then, with halting steps, she stepped up to the beautiful door that was now sparkling with a brilliant light. Carefully, she put the key into the door and turned it.

The door opened, and a great outpouring of color and music greeted her. She could see many beautiful creatures—elves, fairies, pixies, and many more tiny beings—in an array of colorful dress jumping up and down. They all smiled at her and sang this pretty little song:

"Helpful lady,
we welcome you here!
Step through the door
and bring you near!"

So the now very old lady stepped through the door. As she did, a remarkable thing happened. All of the wrinkles from the woman's face fell to the ground, and she felt her body straightening and surging with a vitality of long ago. She was no longer old, but had been transformed into the young woman she had once been!

Following this amazing change, a small delegation of smiling elves stepped forward. In unison, they sang out, "Welcome to the Wonders of Fairy Land! Your many helpful acts have not gone unnoticed! You have earned the right to stay with us as long as you wish!"

Then one of the elves unrolled a document that went on and on. He announced with great authority, "See! Here is the list of all that you have done!"

With this presentation, all of the inhabitants of Fairy Land were now singing together as if they were a symphony, "You are a very helpful person! It is time for us to serve you!" Then they all began to do many sweet things for the now young woman. Two pixies fetched her a comfortable chair to sit upon. A fairy brought her a buttercup full of sweet nectar, and then another fairy brought her a whole plateful of special fairy cakes. And while all this was going on, the lady was entertained by dancing and singing fairy folk of every kind.

The woman's spirits soared! Never had she felt so much joy. She now fully realized that her life had been well spent. Her effort to help others was appreciated!

The End

Epilogue

Dear Reader, this brings us to the end of my collection of stories. Thank you for taking the time to read them. I hope they have both entertained and informed you about some of the many ups and downs of life. The best to you.

Linda Champion

About the Author

Linda Champion is a retired high school teacher who taught for twenty years in the Sacramento area. She lives with her husband, Kenneth Champion, in Citrus Heights, California, and enjoys spending time with family members and friends. One of her favorite things is hosting a candlelight dinner party, which usually leads to some lively conversation. She also offers the use of her antique-filled "Rose Room" and "Emerald Room" to overnight visitors. And sometimes Linda throws in a tune on her violin. *Fairy Tales for Life: A Collection of Fourteen Original Short Stories* is Linda's second literary effort. Her first book is entitled *Conversations with My Auntie Margaret about Sporty Dog.* Both books can be purchased at www.ChampionWritingCreations.com.

About the Illustrator

In her own words, Rose Fante describes herself as "a loyal friend and a hardworking momma." She is the mother of a ten-year-old son. In further describing herself, she says, "I like to think I live my art." And it is obvious that she does, judging from her many drawings and photographs.

I first met Rose through my stepson, Nathan Champion. At the time, I was looking for someone who could draw a dog, the focus of my first book, *Conversations with My Auntie Margaret about Sporty Dog.* To my delight, she was able to capture the personality of this rambunctious, but friendly, dog.

Later, when I completed work on my second book, *Fairy Tales for Life: A Collection of Fourteen Original Short Stories*, Rose was again my choice for illustrator. She told me that she would make my tales come to life, and she did! With two books completed, Rose plans to pursue a career as an illustrator. If you would like to discuss a future project with her, you can reach her through my website at www.ChampionWritingCreations.com.

Thanks, Rose, for your beautiful drawings!

Linda Champion